THE MAGPIE FUNERAL

ALSO BY ADAM J. GALANSKI-DE LEÓN

Szarotka (forthcoming 2024)

The Magpie Funeral

Adam J. Galanski-De León

QUERENCIA

Querencia Press, LLC
Chicago Illinois

QUERENCIA PRESS

© Copyright 2023
Adam J. Galanski-De León

ISBN: 978 1 959118 72 5

www.querenciapress.com

First Published in 2023

Querencia Press, LLC
Chicago IL

Printed & Bound in the United States of America

For Stan

I am dreaming of a dead magpie bedded in a garden of purple crocuses. And I see this magpie, torn feathers, a grim plumage of black and white sullied with dirt. Its beak is in the air, sharp and slit open like a pair of scissors, tongue wretched in a frozen curve under the gold carnation sky. I see this magpie, and I know something terrible is about to happen to him.

***

Jan is being chased through the cobblestone streets of Krakow. The footsteps break the quiet of the night. There are men following him with knives, guns, and barking dogs held tight by chains.

Jan owes gambling debts to these men. It is money he did not have to gamble in the first place. He passes the stone turrets of Wawel Castle on the winding hill. A trumpet sounds the hour from St. Mary's Basilica in the Old Town Market Square. The dogs are let off their chained leashes. Jan breaks for the rocky shore of the Wisła River. Without looking back, he dives in. Swimming across the current, he struggles for breath. The yapping hounds and grunting of angry men echo with the trumpet's dreary notes through the brooding darkness lit by scattered streetlamps.

***

I wake up and Jan is in his garden, tending to the crocuses. It relieves my nocturnal dread. I watch him through the cross sections of the four-paneled bedroom windows. A crooked grin draws upon my face. Nothing's funny. Just curious.

Two magpies flutter from the wind-blown boughs of a golden larch and perch upon the shoulders of his heavy canvas jacket. Jan only acknowledges them with a two-toned whistle,

11

and a double smooching kiss of his pursed lips dropped back into a natural frown. His eyes are the ice of a mountain river. One real and blue. One taken and replaced with white hazed glass.

The depth of his stare is endless, like that of a shark, though his pupil doesn't presume to be focused on much of anything. With a strain of his back, he bends to pat his hands on the soil. The magpies maintain their balance just the same, as more tag along to observe. They anxiously squawk and nip at each other in the overgrown browning blades of grass curled orange with shedding foliage, like children waiting through an adult formality to play.

I slide back down under the wool blanket decorated with images of sienna leaves and filagree, identical to the ones slung over racks and sold in stalls by vendors in the marketplace of Krupówki Street that I browsed, eyeing the various hides, furs, and leathers when I first arrived to town. The four walls of the bedroom, much like the rest of the rooms of Jan's chalet, are natural pine wood panels, with beams crossing under the ceiling, carved with mirrored designs of Carpathian flora above a floor adorned with bear skin, wooden nightstand, open suitcase, and dresser.

I roll over and peer back out the window towards the neighboring building. The red tin shingles of the roof stick out like a tourist from the once natural wood colored siding of the cottage, now faded dark with the passing of arduous winters. The base of the house is composed of gray stone carved much like the support beams of the bedroom in which I lay. Lost in the trance of the morning calm, I hardly notice Jan has gone. Only the tiding of magpies remains. They peck at the freshly watered earth around the garden, ripping flailing insects from under the canopy of the violet petals.

I stretch and yawn, my vision blurred. Then a monotone voice, "Come with me. We forage mushrooms now." I rub my eyes and see him standing in the doorway, clutching a flat-bottomed wicker basket weaved tightly like cords shoved together in a junk cupboard drawer. His broad shoulders rival Frankenstein's monster. Tumbleweeds of wiry hair protrude from his ears in gray tufts. A derelict version of a regal Maine Coon.

His foggy glass eye reminds me of a crystal ball. There is a mystery shrouded in it. A glimpse of the future. Something only he knows. Not meant for me to see. He knows I am staring, but doesn't seem to care.

"I'll get dressed." I tell him. He makes no move to walk away. At first, I think he doesn't comprehend. Not having had to use English in years. But I see there is something troubled in the way he continues to examine me. It is why he lingers. I'm a buried memory. A faded scar rediscovered. An aberration in the smoothness of naked skin. I see the haunting realization in one's own image if you take the time to hold your stare too intensely within a mirror.

***

Jan leads me alongside a river curling around protruding rock faces, through the forest of the Dolina Białego, the white valley at the base of Zakopane's mountain peaks. "Why mushrooms?" I ask him, uncertain if he can hear me. He is ten feet ahead, digging his walking stick into the dirt with one hand,

and wicker basket swinging loosely in the other. In the distance I can see the weeping shower and spraying mist of a waterfall past the oncoming wooden bridge.

A brown buzzard with gold talons and hooked beak caws and swoops into the tree line, descending like a warplane upon the scattering mice and voles. From the brush a black cat rushes across our path with its tail puffed like a feather duster in retreat. A stray. Jan pays no mind to any of this. He browses the base of the tree trunks and makes his way further up the trail.

"It is autumn. So, we look for mushrooms." He tells me, now even farther ahead. "Some we dry. Some we freeze. But all we will eat. Though, I must show you which ones are poison." I look up to the highest peak. Wielki Giewont. The arch of the mountain takes the shape of the brow ridge and nose of a man. Across the range, more peaks form the shape of the mouth and body. "The sleeping knight," Jan says. Only then do I realize he is watching me. He has turned to let me catch up. "Knight of the mountains said to protect Poland when in danger." I chuckle at this, imagining an oafish golem crumbling off the face of the mountain to stretch his limbs and swing his unwieldly stone sword across the clouds. Jan does not see the humor. He begins walking again before I can join his side.

The trail takes a steeper incline. I trip on roots and rocks, slip in mud, catch my face on branches, but Jan doesn't falter. He kneels at the base of a spruce tree and removes a group of lanky mushrooms with thin saucer caps opened like umbrellas, tossing them in his basket. "Parasol," he tells me without looking away from his work. "Edible." He groans standing up. I move to help him, but do so in vain.

Once again, we hike upward, past purple bellflowers, alpine poppies, monkshoods protruding from green stems with petals of perfect indigo. Higher up in the pines Jan finds penny buns, brown caps six inches wide with thick white stalks, hanging off the gray bark like puffing tumors. He picks these while I examine the mountain houseleeks, clustered rosettes of green leaves adorned with reddish floral stars, gnats and mosquitos spiraling above.

He shows me the creamy fluid of the milk caps when cut from the dirt. The poisonous toadstools of the fly amanita, bright red, sickly dotted with cloudy white. We smell a carrion rot and Jan assures me it is a mushroom, not an animal. A phallic stemmed Stinkhorn with a bulbous head, nauseous green. "Not desirable," he shakes his head in pity.

I hear the love song of flirting wallcreepers playing tag off a stone formation and between the boughs of a rowan teaming with scarlet berries. I marvel at the contrast of their gray bodies, with stark red and dark brown feathers, patterned with circles the hue of pearls. We are at a height where we can see the landscapes of the neighboring mountains wearing October treetops like a coat of sheep's wool dyed amber, swaying in the howl of the wind. "Look," says Jan. He points towards a nearby ridge where two chamois graze, one tan, one black, hooked horns protruding between oval ears, stiff and alert.

Jan brings me to a wall of rock. He begins to scale it, slowly, careful not to spill his wicker basket which is now filled to the brim with a variety of mushrooms and even some stems of alpine flora. "Where are you going?" I ask him. The air is chilled at this elevation, but I am sweating, now realizing how long it has been since I have truly exercised. "What's up there?"

Jan's silence entices me to pursue. I wipe my face with the sleeve of my coat, find a foothold and begin to climb. I can't believe he can scale this cliff face at such an age, while for me it is a constant breathless struggle. As I am halfway up the rockface, I look up to see Jan hurling himself onto the next plateaued surface with a laborious grunt. A penny bun drops from his basket and bounces off my forehead, smushing into the dirt below. I almost slip. At the top of the wall, Jan grabs my hand and helps pull me across. "Where am I?" I wheeze, hands, knees, and head pressed into the rubble of dirt and stone.

"Sarnia Skala," Jan tells me. When he realizes these words don't process, he says in a more commanding tone, "Just look. The mountain peak." I prop myself up and to one side of the range, the sleeping knight of the mountain is closer than ever before. A quilt of trees below me stretching endlessly into the distance. Thick rows of pines spreading higher above. And across the open air, the ski slopes, the rolling patchwork fields of rural countryside, the nameless dirt roads and meandering trails. The town of Zakopane. And somewhere within it, Jan's home.

"It's beautiful," I tell him. "It's amazing."

"Yes. Yes," Jan nods. The conversation goes no further. I am busy taking in the sights. Hawks circle the ridge. Their cries echo in the empty space. Jan looks me curiously up and down.

"So, tell me," he breaks the silence. "Why are...you here?"

The bell of a blue willow gentian he has plucked sweeps from his basket and soars off the cliff face into the open sky. There it is a teardrop in the endless blue. I face him, squinting, flash a smile that he does not return, run my fingers through my windblown hair, and reply.

"I was hoping to ask you that exact question."

***

Long gone are the days in the Lenin Steel Plant of Nowa Huta. Trains and ships were granted safe passage by the grace of the Queen Virgin Mary. But still, labor is the language of the world.

Jan is working in the powder mill on the Monongahela River, outside of Pittsburgh, Pennsylvania, USA. He stands by a sputtering dynamite truck. It idles, waiting to be loaded. On both sides of the trailer bold paint reads "DANGEROUS EXPLOSIVES" above the name of the company. Jan wipes the sweat off his brow and puffs a cigarette, leaning into the steel of the rumbling vehicle. Inside the mill, coworkers toil grinding and mixing charcoal, saltpeter, and sulfur to be packed into barreled kegs.

Jan snuffs his cigarette into the dirt with a twist of his leather boot. He looks up into the sky. Gray clouds dampen the sun. The river reeks of sulfur and flows a murky brown. Autumnal leaves pile along its banks. The subdued chatter of men speaking a language Jan hardly understands harmonizes with the repetitive buzzing and clanking of machinery.

Jan's shoulders flinch in shock. A crack sounds out in the mill, followed by shouts, and the resounding boom of an explosion that shakes the ground, quakes the trees, rings all ears within distance, and heaves him forward into the dirt. Psia krew! Dog's blood! Flaming debris is projected into the air, lighting fire to the foliage of the riverside. Jan covers his head as chunks of metal and wood pummel the ground beside him. Men shout and cry. Jan knows not the words but understands their meaning.

He chokes for breath and enters the smoke and flames of the mill's inferno. It is almost too dark to see, so Jan moves by the shouts around him. The ceiling has caved in. Doorways are blocked with debris. He approaches the wailing voices, reaching out to a hand in the smoldering mist. He drags another man's body towards him, hoists it, and carries.

Jan helps three men out of the powder mill this way. By the time he can go back in for the fourth, the fire department has arrived and is on the situation. Jan sits by the river, covered in ash, face blackened with smoke. He washes his shirt in the murky waters, dips his cupped hands and splashes some onto his forehead, rubbing his cheeks and throat. A man approaches him.

"Christ, pal. I saw what you did back there! You're a goddam hero, buddy. Outta your mind, but a hero. Say, what's your name?"

Jan looks at the man with a blank face, trying to pick apart the words between his foreign accent. The man stares at Jan expectantly, receiving no answer to his question. He shrugs and turns to walk away as a deep raspy voice chokes out a response behind him.

"I am Jan."

***

Jan is a man of few words and even fewer answers. The day's walk back down the mountain was spent in general silence. As I leave his home for Krupówki Street, he hardly acknowledges me. He is busy tossing birdseed to the magpies on his lawn. He hums them a tune and in return they squawk for more, dancing in their tuxedos of black wings and white undersides. He is a celebrity to them. And to him they are his friends. Their corvid screeches cut the side street's tranquility the same as rusty sawblades in a dilapidated barn house lining the edge of a Lawrence County road.

Chalets and alpine cottages give way to back streets and narrow alleyways. The main strip of town is cut off to through traffic save the pedestrians on foot and tourists parading in horse drawn carriages, steered by wool clad Gorals donning leather hats and capes, crops and reins gripped tight within their palms.

I weave through the crowd past dumpling shops, hostels, winter sport stores, and vendors selling knock-offs of authentic Goral clothing. Squeezed between a drug store, labeled "Apteka," and a mountain tourism office, is a slice of American culture. An H & M outlet with expansive glass windows revealing posh vacationing families browsing for sweaters and last-minute winter coats.

A savory smell carries on the wind and I am drawn to the restaurant display window where breaded pork knuckles, *golonka*, ham hock the size of softballs, sizzle in their own fats in a curved iron skillet. I can taste the richness on my tongue. The tenderness. The salt.

My appetite is killed at the next window, a bakery, where paczki have sat out all day and are now infiltrated with a swarm of yellow jackets, crawling in and out of the doughnut's crème filling and frosting. Some buzz into the window pane, drunken with sugar. Others are trapped in the goo of the paczki's innards, wings destroyed and unable to flutter, twitching their mandibles and antennae while making peace with their hedonistic death.

Next is a row of benches. A man plays a shoddy acoustic guitar and sings in a throaty voice under a dying tree, while an old caricature artist in a metal folding chair uses charcoal to sketch the smiling image of a young man and his father. In this rendition their facial features somehow morph into near resemblances of the artist himself. He shows his work and their smiles shift into confused side glances.

On this strip of benches is also the first group of bums I've seen since I arrived in town. They drink honey cordial and bimber out of nips and have a six pack of Tatra lager split between them. They stare down the passing tourists with self-righteous sneers as they drink, but make no move towards true confrontation.

They are not the bums sometimes found in major American cities. The kind who will smoke cigarettes indoors and blow it in your face. Attack you on the bus without warning. Masturbate at meek teenage girls sitting alone with their legs crossed and headphones on in a Tuesday evening train car. Or stab rich college kids and leave them bleeding under streetlamps with their pockets empty, hanging off the sides of designer blue jeans. Yes, these highlanders' shoulders slouch. Their brains are wet. Clothes tattered. Faces ugly, spotted with scars and sores from use of hard drugs. But the aggression is not there. Just the dark stains on their trousers and stream of piss trickling down their legs into the glass of the bottles smashed upon the pavement's slabs of stone.

On the corner of Sanktuarium Najświętszej Rodziny, on Jan Paweł II Street, I stop at a stall and purchase a block of oscypek, smoked sheep cheese pressed in conical shapes with diamond patterns, some dusted with paprika, others paired with cranberry marmalade to dip. Next to the oscypek are longer stringed strands of cheese labeled kobarcik, and combs and spreads of honey. More stalls of local vendors are set up on this end of Krupówki. They sell wood-carved and hand painted matryoshka, ceramic beer steins, red slippers embroidered with white edelweiss, leather goods, fur hats and coats. There is taxidermy, boar skin rugs with claws and snout still attached. Fox pelt mats. And woolen blankets designed with brown leaves as in Jan's cottage. I think to buy him something. Something to break the ice. To show I care. But I pass another stall, selling outdated rock band t-shirts, and clothing with tacky phrases. The kind I'd find at a Spencer's Gifts in a shopping mall back home. I wonder how many of these stalls seem just as tacky to the locals as they do to me and decide it might just be better to head back up the road.

A cacophony of screaming birds, and my eyes turn to a business almost the size of a shed where parents are paying for their children to sip apple juice and feed seeds to massive parrots, macaws, and cockatoos. Their vibrant tropical plumage is blinding compared to the evergreens, grays, and umber pallets of these alpine forests where the coming snow will blanket the ranges white and only prove even further that their flaring rainbow torsos weren't made to belong in the mundane.

This image draws a sadness deep from the well of my heart. A sadness I know can only be quenched with alcohol as I walk back up Krupówki eyeing the patios of log house pubs where bands of Gorals compete for attention wearing traditional garb and instruments slung across their bodies. Violins and cellos. Some with accordions. Glissando voices lyricized and harmonized in a Gwara tongue. Groups of young men and woman dining on gulasz, silesian dumplings, or spreads of trout, sing along with the Podhale music, albeit offkey, brimming with nostalgia, and pride, for the uneducated onlookers to consider with wondrous stares.

I cut down an alleyway, searching for something quiet. A slow burn. Alone in this foreign land. Trying to rekindle a connection that maybe was never there. To a man as peculiar to me as the mountain culture that I find hard to understand. I see light in a window. *Café Piano*, it reads. I push the door and enter into the shadows of the candle-lit calm.

***

It is three in the morning in Newcastle, Pennsylvania. Jan sits on his couch. His face is illuminated by the glow of television. John Wayne is on. In the room behind him, Jan's wife snores under her bed sheets, with their young son cradled in her arms. Nightmares again. So, they share a mattress.

Jan has no nightmares. He drinks cheap bourbon and watches John Wayne well into the morning. Sometimes he pours a bourbon shot straight into a pint glass of Iron City Beer. He laughs at the television but he doesn't know why. Here and there he picks up phrases. "Well, howdy, Pilgrim! You can't serve papers on a rat, baby sister! Young fella, if you're looking for trouble, I'll accommodate you!" But his favorite lines out of all the westerns are during the gunfights. "Draw!" They shout this before firing off their pistols at ten paces away. Jan says this to his son when they play, in a fake American accent. He pulls the triggers to his finger guns and leans in to swoop his boy into the air, laughing.

The pint glass looks small in Jan's bear paw hands, puffed thick with callouses. He sips and pours more and chuckles, at the voices, the postures, the outfits. Some of the cowboy's ensembles remind Jan of the Polish Highlanders. He closes his eyes and imagines the Tatras, hums an old melody. Muzyka Góralska. This conjures nostalgia. And then a sadness. But before Jan can embrace the sadness, he has woken up on the couch during the morning light. The TV is still on. The local weather reports. His glass is spilled and empty on the floor. A new dark stain adorns the carpet like a Rorschach. Jan never knew he was asleep. The perfect way to avoid bad dreams.

***

Inside Café Piano, an upright nurses the chipped paint wound of the entryway wall. Above it, grayscale photographs are hung by cheap wire on nails that sag like heavy earrings from the weight against the plaster. The black and white keys are faded with habitual wear. The fingers that move like spiders. The creeping sharps and flats that complement the rattling of ice within a rocks glass. Jazz keyboard swoons from the corner speakers by the ceiling, giving the upright a ghostly aura. A sound heard, but no player seen. A song fit for the roaring twenties without an audience to receive it.

At the perimeter of the room, coffee tables, wrinkled leather sofas, wooden chairs, and potted plants sprouting off yellow-green. Candles at every surface, flickering orange, shaded by the curves of olive-hued glass holders. The light just dim enough to disguise the stains on the tile floor to the unfocused eye. A sliding glass door to a lifeless back patio. Chairs stacked up for the evening.

The bar counter, the three sides of a perfect square. Where the square would close, the back bar's bottles of assorted vodkas, brandies, cordials, and mainstream American whiskies, give way to the open stock room and kitchen station of refrigerated fruits and garnishes, boxes of cleaning supplies, and packs of domestic beer. The counter is lined with wooden swings, a few feet from the ground, tethered to the ceiling by pairs of thick rope secured by mountaineering equipment, such as carabineers among other hooks.

In a far swing by the bathroom door a man sits sipping vodka. His hair is thin and cut short, almost buzzed, receding in a steep widow's peak. He appears brawny in the collared shirt too tight for him. The top two buttons are undone to reveal black-brown tumbleweeds curling from the pale of his skin. He is speaking Polish to the young woman bartender, muddling berries in a mason jar with a smooth tool of wood.

She looks down at her work. Dirty blonde wavy hair hanging in her face. She nods revealing a modest palette of make-up. A natural look. As she mushes the berries to the bottom of her glass, the bracelets shake up and down her wrist, muted by the cuffs of her green flannel, which she wears open against the red cloth of her low-cut undershirt. She nods again, this time at me, and I scramble to remember the Polish crash course I gave myself in preparation for the trip.

"Dzień dobry. Jak się masz?" I ask quietly in hopes of hiding my poor annunciation below the sound of the music. I sit down at a swing, ass swaying clumsily until I properly plant my feet on the runner below the counter. The bartender says something to me that I understand, only out of context clues, to be a question of what I would like to drink. "Poproszę, jednego dużego Żywce," I recite an order I google-translated earlier in the day. She puts a tall glass to the taps and pours me one large Żywiec lager. She says the price and I struggle with the bills in my wallet before throwing on the bar top what I realize to be the wrong amount of cash, only when she shakes her head, smiles, and hands me back half of my zloty. At the far swing, her male friend shrugs and laughs.

"Co to jest?" *What is this?* I ask her, pointing towards the mashed berries. She pivots to the back bar and retrieves a kettle steaming with hot water.

"Herbata," she says with the ghost of a smile on her lips, and I now realize she is preparing tea.

Three young girls enter the café. They are maybe nineteen or twenty. Each filled with more life than the three of us at the bar combined. They are well manicured, hair straightened flat, up in a bun, or tied in a pony tail with an elastic band. Their speech is bubbly. How I imagine a valley girl would talk if she grew up in the Tatras. The bartender exudes a Zen-like calm contrasted against the bouncing pitches of their voices. She pours them three Żywiec and grabs bottles of syrups, dripping drops of different fruit flavoring into each of the pints.

The girls pay their zloty and sit on a sofa at a coffee table in the back of the room. Their chattering accompanies the swinging keys and noodling leads of the piano through the speakers. I am left in silence, observing the buff man and his glass of vodka. Then this bartender, who I realize now to be very beautiful in a small-town sort of sense. I feel arrogant for that thought to have crossed my mind. But still, I wish to talk to her. Make myself known.

From a beam above the bar, various bottles are stationed upside down with fitted pour spouts that I recognize are made to pour exactly an ounce at one time. The bottles themselves are unfamiliar. The bartender catches me staring and addresses me in Polish too fast to comprehend. I clear my throat, and apologize, tossing to the side the rouse that I speak her native tongue.

"Sorry. I don't know how to say it in Polish. But can I try some of this? This...Spirytus?"

"Ha!" Caws the man down the bar with a cocksure smirk. "You are going to end up in hospital if you drink that garbage!" The bartender laughs with him but motions towards me as if not to listen.

"What's wrong with it?" I ask.

"That stuff will destroy your stomach! It's over 190 proof. It's made for bums. You need to grow up drinking it, or you might puke out your innards."

"Is it really that bad?" I ask the bartender. "I'm not new to drinking by any means."

"It does not have a good taste, I must say," she laughs. "But if you want to try it, I will pour you one."

"Sure, why not?"

"You are going to regret it! I tell you, don't waste your time," says the man. He throws down some zloty on the bar and says his farewell to the young woman. He puts his hand on my shoulder walking past and looks to the bartender. "I just saved your customer's life!" Then to me, "Hey man, I know you think you are a tough guy. But no. Seriously, have a good night." My eyes follow him out the door, waiting for it to creak and then slam behind him.

"Is it really *that* bad?"

"He is exaggerating. Just try some," she says. She reaches to the beam where the bottle of Spirytus is hanging upside down and pulls an ounce from the spout into a small glass. She places it in front of me, and I can immediately smell its foulness. Like a cleaning supply or rubbing alcohol. I pull the glass to my lips, the bartender examining me throughout the process. I wet my tongue with one sip. A burning, stinging sensation of a sip. The taste of gasoline. Immediately after swallowing I hack the cough of a lifelong smoker into the elbow of my jacket which I have instinctually pulled up to my mouth. She is laughing at me. My cheeks flush red.

"Here," she tells me. She reaches for her kettle of hot water and pours another glass of herbata filled with muddled wild berries. "Come on. Give me your glass." She motions. I hand her the spirytus and she dumps it into the mug she has prepared, diluting it into the tea. She uses an extended bar spoon to swirl around the mixture with spastic, syncopated clinks, her bracelets sliding up and down her wrist. When she is done, she hands it to me. "Be careful. It's hot," she warns with a tenderness in her voice.

I put the tea to my lips and take a gentle pull. "Much better. So much tastier." I laugh. And now she laughs with me. "I must ask."

"Mhm?"

"My Polish...Is it very bad?" She shrugs and looks off at the young women gossiping by the back wall. Their voices raise sharp and laughter strikes like lighting.

"It is not so bad." She offers, "But I could tell you are not from here if that is what you are saying."

"No. I am definitely not from here." I lower my head and stare down into red berries floating in the murky water of my herbata.

"Then where?" she asks, pulling her cup of tea to her mouth cradled in either palm.

"From the States. Pennsylvania. Outside of Pittsburgh. You know it?"

"Yes. I know it. Of it, at least. And what do you do there?"

"I teach writing at a community college. Creative writing." Her eyes light up at this.

"Oh, so you are a writer?" I put my hands up in a modest shrug.

"Well, I am trying to be. Teaching writing often leaves no time to write for myself."

"And I assume this is why you are here? Across the world. To find the story?"

"Partially. To be honest, I'm here to see an old relative. A man I haven't seen since I was a kid. I wasn't even sure if he'd still be here. Or be alive. But I think…you know…I think the story I want to write is somewhere in there."

"The best stories come from true life experience. So maybe this is true what you say." She assures.

"Yeah? How do you figure?"

"I am a writer too."

"And you work here?"

"Obviously."

"But did you go to school?"

"Not more than a semester in Krakow."

"You should go back!" I slap my hand on the counter, "A young writer, you should be involved in academia." My heart drops when she rolls her eyes.

"I like to remind myself that Bukowski worked in a post office for many years of his life."

"Ha! And what do you know of Mr. Bukowski?" As I say this, I can tell I have come on too strong. She shoots me a paused look of disgust before continuing the conversation.

"What do I know? Why? Because I'm a girl?"

"No, no...I'm sorry. I mean, he is a very American writer."

"I think you might assume what I know or don't know based on how you perceive my job. Or this town. For example, what do you know of great Polish writers? Tokarczuk, Szymborska, Miłosz, Twardoch?"

"I admit I don't know much of anything."

"I figured as much," she sips her tea with an air of self-satisfaction. And now I feel like the greatest fool.

"Look, miss..."

"Basia."

"Basia," I repeat, thinking it to be a pretty name. "I did not intend to offend you. I'm sorry if I came off as arrogant."

"It's all right. I assumed as much once you told me you were American." My face flushes red once more.

The three young girls come up to the bar and order another round of beer and flavored syrup. When they draw back to their table, Basia and I are left in an uncomfortable silence.

"Thank you again for the tea," I nod. "It makes this so much easier to drink."

"No problem. That man, Mateusz, my customer. He likes to act like he never learned the hard way either."

"If it's not too forward," I say after downing the remainder of my cup, "Maybe we could meet up and talk writing sometime. I'm on leave from work and will be in Zakopane for a bit. I don't know anyone here, besides my grandfather, Jan. It would be nice to chat. Maybe grab some food." From my coat I pull a pen, click it, and jot my information down on a bar napkin. "Here is my number, if you are interested."

"I'll consider it," she takes the napkin from my grip, and says coyly, "It could be fun, talking writing, that is. With an American. I haven't written in a bit. It seems we could both use some inspiration..."

Now it is her turn to follow me out the door with her eyes, as I lift myself off the swing and stumble across the room, the effect of the spirytus hitting harder now that I am on my feet. She smiles and shakes her head, fully understanding. I wave bashfully, avoiding her gaze, pass the lonely piano and through the door out into the alley where the sounds of Krupówki fade in with the glare of the streetlamps, and the jaunt of the keyboard decays into the groan of the wind.

***

"What do you call them in Polish?" I ask, heaving my axe into the chopping block, cutting into a wood log and stomping it down further with my boot to split the piece in half. In the Tatras, autumn is short. Winter will come soon and firewood will be important.

"Sroka," says Jan, referring to the magpie on his shoulder. It excitedly flaps its wings, stretching its black beak forward to receive the torn off pieces of bread from Jan's pinched fingers. He makes the usual whistles and kissing noises with his lips and gently strokes the bird's head down to its beak. The little beast's eyes are beady and vacant. Still, the connection is visible.

"Sroka..." I mimic his accent, attempting to gently roll the "r" as he did, so effortlessly. "And how did you get to be so close with them?"

"They were always here," Jan tosses a log at my feet. Another magpie swoops from the drooping boughs of the larch, pale gold, bark brittle, graying, half naked of its leaves. "As long as my family has owned this house they have been here, this tiding. We give them things. Food, water, flowers in the garden. Affection. But they also like odd things. Shiny things."

I wipe sweat from my brow, lean my axe against the stained wood of the chalet, and look to the magpie that has landed amidst the fading saffron of the crocuses, their stems leaning in the breeze which wafts the smoke of nearby bon fires, and the richness of homecooked stew from the cottage window cracked for ventilation next door. There is something glistening within the clutches of the magpie's beak. Golden. Perhaps a band with a diamond. It reflects the setting rays of the marmalade sun back into the rose petal hues of gray cumulus heaps that float in the no-man's-land between the trenches of night and day.

"How do you say in English?" Jan asks, approaching the bird in the garden. The magpie on his shoulder flaps its wings and retreats to the red tin shingles of the neighboring roof, another piece of bread dangling from its mouth. "Hair-loom?"

"Oh, *heirloom*," I correct him, chuckling. The magpie is squawking, wrestling with the shiny object in the dirt.

"Yes. They also like to steal my *heirlooms* from time to time," Jan says. He leans down with a groan, and scoops the thrashing magpie up by its torso. It calms in his arms. The sweep of its wings dies down like it was done with the turned dial of a ceiling fan. Soon there is no motion. Just curious chirps. The bird drops the diamond ring into Jan's open palm. He holds it up to his face and examines it for scuff marks. Then he slips it in the breast pocket of his canvas jacket and buttons it shut. Jan strokes the *sroka* on the top of the head, rubs its belly, and feeds it a portion of bread. It bubbles and coos in satisfaction, clutching at his fingers with its toes to hang upside down and stretch its wings. Their dynamic is sublime, Jan, and this tiding of birds that have lived alongside his family for generations.

"You have more wood to chop, no?" Jan turns to me. "Soon it will snow. And we will require a fire." He makes his way back into his cottage, taking caution not to trip on the slabs of stone that act as his front steps. I nod, and grip the handle of my axe tight in both hands, scanning my eyes from Jan to the magpies, suddenly struck with a searing flame of jealousy.

***

Jan's son is playing with toy soldiers in the front yard, whistling like a fluttering bird. Rain fell the night before and the grass remains damp. The fabric of his blue Levi's is wetted with a darker hue from the dew on his knees pressed into the lawn. Through the front window of the house, Jan's wife washes dishes in the kitchen sink, scrubbing bubbles onto ceramic plates with a white rag.

"Żabko," Jan calls to his son, appearing from behind a tree, holding a .22 rifle. "Piotr! Little Froggie..."

Piotr looks up from his toy soldiers to his grinning father who beckons him to stand up. "The toys, Żabko. Put them down."

Piotr drops the soldiers, and Jan puts a real gun in the grip of his child, then straightens the rifle to a proper shooting posture in his arms. "Dobrze. See, now aim," Jan tells him, guiding the barrel of the gun towards his wife washing dishes in the window.

"Tato, I'm scared," Piotr whimpers.

"It not real gun, Froggie. See? Make pull trigger..." Once again, Jan guides his son's hands. Piotr slides his fingers on the trigger. With an abrasive pop, the gun recoils back, knocking him on the ground. In the same moment the front window to the house shatters with the break of a bullet. Inside, Jan's wife screams bloody murder. Her plate falls and smashes to pieces on the yellow linoleum floor. The bullet has missed. Piotr lays in the wet grass crying. The bottom of his pants is now stained with dew. Jan's wife gets up and howls in Polish out the busted window, but it is too late.

Jan is dashing through the yard like a frightened deer. He runs through the entire neighborhood past maple trees, gray houses, and rusted cars parked by pot holes and overgrown lawns. He doesn't stop running until he is deep in the woods on the edge of the neighborhood. Here he hides behind the trees, slunk down where the trunks meet the dirt, listening to the echoing threats and curses of his wife scaring the crows out from the upper boughs.

Jan returns from the woods in the light of the early morning. His wife awakes and he is met at the front door with the flailing wooden end of a broom.

***

When I left Pittsburgh, it was sunset. We flew into the darkness with the remaining rose of daylight soaking into the

34

edge of the black. I watched the sprawl of the city lights below us disgorge into the vacant industrial towns of the mountains. To calm my nerves, I drank cognac and ate. A meal, and then nip after nip until I fell fast asleep.

When I woke, the flight tracker screen showed we were crossing Denmark, near Copenhagen, high above the cloud lining. The lights were off in the cabin. When I slid open my window a weak stream of light shown across the faces of the snoring passengers. A sizzling ball, a red lump of charcoal burned beneath the clouds. And I realized it to be the sun. Where we had left it behind us in America, here we were chasing its rise on the other side of the world. Within minutes the red bulb rose and the whole sky was a wisping pastel pink and orange. Like catholic frescoes. It was enough to assure myself in the importance of my journey,

I spent one day in Krakow. In the Old Town Square, I watched brides in flowing white be photographed next to their grooms in front of the towers of St. Mary's Basilica, while penguin-clothed nuns made their way to the chapel in droves, heads bowed like the corners of their lips. I walked down the hill to Wawel Castle, observing the streets raised from the days of no public sanitation, the trash building up and paved over and over through the years, until the first floors became basements below the sidewalk, and the second floors became public entryways.

On the shores of the Vistula I ate a whole herring on a river boat and drank vodka with long names I couldn't pronounce. Bicyclists zipped by on the two-lane trail hugging the water. I picked at the divots of my kluski śląskie potato dumplings spread with pesto sauce and cherry tomatoes, feeling almost as an imposter. Someone undercover. A man who shouldn't be across the world, but in doing so has disguised himself and blended in the maze of a foreign city. A number in the mass of people. Muted by the barrier of language. And in this revelation, if at least for a brief moment, I felt truly free.

Then the Kazimierz neighborhood, the old Jewish Ghetto with Klezmer musicians on the corner playing sharp sad songs on violins, some with brass instruments or clarinets. The buildings frowned in dilapidation compared to the tourist attraction decadence of the market square. The pubs were claustrophobic, cluttered tight with tables and chattering young people. The buildings' interiors seemingly as old as the city itself. I left for an outdoor market and ate a zapiekanki, open faced sandwich on a long paper tray, sitting on a curb, watching all the people pass by, feeling a mixture of total anxiousness and wonder.

By nightfall I walked back to the main square, finding my way by the circular park path that surrounds it. I walked cobblestone roads past pubs, bakeries, handmade pottery storefronts, and tourist shops. Women of the street stopped to greet me. Botox injected lips, plump like worms. Plastic faces of human barbie dolls overdone with makeup. Long blonde hair straightened. Revealing clothes hugging their curves. *Would you like a drink, gentleman?* They beckoned, *Come. Come with me. Would you like to see my kitty cat world?*

The horn went off in the highest turret of the basilica, the trumpet player playing the same song on every hour to every corner of the world. The song cut one note short each time in remembrance of the day an archer of the invading Mongol horde pierced the throat of the trumpeter with an arrow in the midst of him sounding out the alarm. Crowds stood taking videos with their phones. Musicians played in the streets and people danced. I meandered down an alley and then a discrete staircase leading under the ground where I watched a trio play their first of two sets in a tiny jazz club, while my eyelids drooped in a heavy daze. In a dreamlike state, I retired to my hostel, listening to the hustle of the streets and the hooligans singing football chants well into the morning calm.

And the morning sky was gray as Pennsylvania, but the vision of the medieval square felt like another world entirely. Some drunks still laid in the street or sprawled out on patio chairs of the restaurants lining the marketplace. Crows sang and hopped from post to post, squabbling for discarded food. Horse-drawn carriages strolled through the mist, hooves clomping on the bricks with the churning groans of the wooden wheels. Their drivers dressed in the garb of traditional Krakowians. Red and black żupan embroidered and worn over a dark vest and billowing white linen undershirt. Trousers held with a leather belt and tucked into high leather boots. Four-cornered krakuska hats, red and black, pierced with long feathers and flowers, and laced with scarlet ribbon.

I met with a chauffeur to take me south to the mountains. And when I stepped inside his car and rode off beyond the confines of the city limits into the rolling countryside, my heart beat faster and my chest pinched tight in nervousness. I couldn't help but think, *what if he isn't there? What if he doesn't want to take me in?*

Days have passed and I am staring into the eyes of a beautiful woman, across a café table, in a shop off of Krupówki, steaming mugs of coffee cradled in our hands. Like a woken somnambulist I struggle to piece together the moments and choices which steered me to this present. I don't know if I believe in fate or more so the supreme randomness of human existence in which we scrape with our claws to find some form of meaning. Either way, with this coffee, in this café, with this woman, in this foreign land, I find my heart soaked with the warmth of deep satisfaction.

Basia smiles with her eyes. She blows on her drink to cool it down. She brushes the hair off her brow and sets it behind her ear. She speaks and her voice is tender.

"So, your grandfather, uh—"

"Jan."

"Jan. He wasn't expecting you?"

"I hadn't talked to him since I was very young. Since he left us to ourselves back in the states." I also blow on my coffee though it fails to cool it down. When I bring it to my lips and gulp, I choke out a wheezing round of coughs.

"But why did he leave?" Basia asks.

"I don't know." I grumble, now half irritated, bumping the gas out of my chest with a clenched fist.

"There had to be a reason," Basia insists, "No one gets up and decides one day to leave their whole family behind."

"I'm still trying to get it out of him. I need him to trust me." I sigh again, sipping from my mug. A group of youths enter the shop and my eyes avert from Basia's, an excuse to relieve my nervousness. "All I know is that something happened between him and my father before he left. There was a rift. One they never opened up to me about, but still exists to this day. It's why my father stayed back in the states instead of coming on this trip."

"If you want him to trust you, you need to be genuine," she looks so confidently into my eyes that my heart winces.

"I am genuine!" I take almost too much offense to her words, and speak this in a tone harsh enough for the expression on her face to reel back in a grimace.

"No, I know. But I mean, in your relationship. Enjoy the time you have to spend with him while you're out here. Bond. While you can. You cannot randomly show up expecting answers to life's questions. In a genuine connection, showing genuine care, you will find your answers. There can be no other way to make him trust you."

I look to Basia with furrowed brows. In response, she nods twice in that self-assured way I have quickly come to both love and hate. In this way she is intimidating to me. And in the back of my mind, I fear she is smarter, though I don't know how it can be at once so daunting and alluring.

"How do you suppose all this?" I challenge. She reaches out and puts her palm on mine and my face flushes red with warmth.

"Listen," Basia says, "I haven't seen my father in a few years. He is away in England working a factory job. The money is better out there. It's worth more out there. He sends it back to my mother every month. Part of me wants answers too. Yes, I respect my father. He is the hardest working man I know. He takes care of our little family. But more than trying to understand why he stays out there, why he never visits, why most of the communication we have with him comes in the form of bank transfers, I appreciate the time I have had to spend with him growing up. The love he showed me. The love that he still shows, just in different ways. Because life does not hand us concrete answers to our troubles. But people show us concrete connections. Bonds. And at the end of the day that gives us more solace, more closure, than any explanation could supply."

"Basia..." I avert my eyes again, pretending to be interested in the conversation at the cash register queue.

"Listen!" She draws me back to her and holds her stare, now more passionate, "I tell you, if my father showed up at my door step tomorrow, I would not waste time questioning his motivations, chastising him for his absence. I would welcome him with the love of open arms!"

"But it's not the same. Jan didn't come out here to support us. He came out here to abandon us."

"And could you stay here in Poland? For the rest of your life? Start a new life and forget your homeland? The house you grew up in? Your grandfather did this in the states. Can you not accept that he possibly missed the world he used to know? He welcomed you with open arms, did he not? It seems to me there is something deeper than abandonment here. Something stronger than longing. Memories of identity. An impulse of the heart. A choice made which you cannot revert, turning back with your tail between your legs. Your grandfather's feelings are not so one-dimensional. And I have a feeling that he is secretly glad you came to visit."

"You act like you know everything," I prod, instantly feeling ashamed of the whininess in my voice.

"And you act like I wouldn't know." She smiles at me and my chest flutters. Her expressions and gestures are a constant rollercoaster. High climbs and low dips that draw a rush of excitement. A feeling of life.

"I like you, Basia. You've got an introspective mind."

"This town breeds introspection. Surrounded by mountain meadows and forest. This winter city. Sometimes we're left with nothing but reverie. Anyway, I thought you wished to talk about writing?"

"The life of a writer is just as interesting," I offer, "For example, how could you only manage one semester in Krakow?"

"I soon learned academia is not for me."

"And how so?"

"Not learning. I love learning. On my own terms. It's the institution that I despise. The academic ladder. Instead of sitting around discussing the mechanics of an art, I'd rather live a life that inspires the production of authentic art. Maybe it won't be so regarded by intellectuals or institutions. But it will be real! I equate it to this—you can sit around and discuss war, politics, and the human history of warfare day in and out, but if you've never been in a battle before, you straddle the border of uselessness in combat. I believe the same goes for art. This is why university is not for everyone. Me, I would rather gain meaningful life experience. Let those who want to study the logistics of prose sit in a classroom!"

"Ha! So, art is combat?" I chuckle and shake my head self-righteously.

"Art is combat. In some ways," she says with a seriousness that quells my smile.

"And you believe working at Café Piano gives you meaningful life experience?"

"It's the foundation for my life story. The inspiration for many of my stories. And it is only the beginning. Or do you think this is all a person like me can amount to?"

"C'mon, Basia, that's not what I meant." I realize she is combative in many more ways than in art, and I find myself to be submissive to women of strong will. More than that, she is starting to convince me. The feeling is as exhilarating and uncomfortable as riding drunk through the city in a reckless taxi.

"You yourself said your academic life made it hard to find time to create!" she counters. "But here you are across the world, away from it. Living. And you have found some form of inspiration! I have dreams to do the same! Maybe I will join my father in England. Labor. Drink. Meet a man. Or woman. Change my way of life. And looking back on these times I spend now in Zakopane, it will all equate to something greater. These small stories of this sleepy town will be the bricks that build the base of an epic."

"We are not so different, Basia."

"It is one of the reasons why I agreed to come here with you." Her eyes say she is telling the truth. I reach in my back pocket, pull out a small notebook and hold it up to her, skimming through the pages with my thumb like a flipbook cartoon.

"I've been documenting my whole trip in this Moleskine. People. Places. Phrases. Streets. Plants and animals. Everything. Like you said you will do someday. I will do the same."

"It is the job of any artist. Documenting your world. Through fact or fiction."

"Your faith in art gives me hope."

"But hope for what?" This time, she is the one drawn to curiosity. I feel an opportunity to say something. Something intelligent. But what comes out feels run of the mill to me compared to the advice Basia so casually drops.

"That this all means something," I say, "That stories are important. That lives are important. My father's, Jan's, and mine. That is all adds up to something. Something bigger than ourselves."

"We are all the gears of a music box. Life's hand winds us tight enough and we have no choice but to release a song. Write that in your little notebook," Basia grins. There is a fire in her eyes, if not for me, then for life itself.

"I will. Oh, I will," I tell her. We sip our coffee, maintaining eye contact, now at a sudden loss for words. She puts her mug down and once again brushes the loose strands of her hair back behind her ears. I decide that when I walk Basia home tonight I will try to kiss her. Her confidence is so contagious that I don't fear the potential embarrassment of being denied.

* *** *

"Rosjanin! Ty Rosjaninie! You bloody Russian! Kurejewka? You were never a Pole! Russian spy!"

Jan's wife is packing her bags to leave. A cab is waiting for her outside. Tears roll down her cheeks. She breaks out in short sniffles while Jan growls. Frustrated by her tenderness, he tries a different approach.

"Serduszko. Sweetheart. Nie chcę Cię stracić. I don't want to lose you. Kocham tylko Ciebie na zawsze! I love only you forever!" Jan moves to hug her and leans his head in for a kiss. His wife growls and smacks him across the face with a thwap. Jan hisses like a cat and grips his cheek, cursing. He hears a feminine whimper and realizes it to be his son crying in the living room. "Mama! Mama! Don't leave!" he sobs. She wipes her eyes and moves to kiss her child on the forehead, then drags her suitcase out the front door. Jan chases after her. By the car, she turns around.

"One last thing!" she says, gripping her fingers. With some effort she slides off her diamond wedding ring and tosses it at Jan's feet. She slams the door to the idling cab and rides down the street, out of the neighborhood. Jan holds the wedding ring up in front of his face, pinched between his fingers. He looks past it into the distance. Piotr cries at his feet.

"Żabko! Froggie, no cry. Stop cry, Froggie." Jan tells him. But there is no way to calm him down.

* *** *

Scarlet and white is the flag of Poland. And such is the blood of the magpie splayed across the trail of paw prints on the

44

new fallen snow. There is a desolation to this winter mountainside. Despite the flame of life on Krupówki Street and the soaring bodies across the winding tourist slopes, the frozen Tatras bear a seductive gloom, voicing the doleful perseverance of the people, of the continually conquered, sprawled naked across history as the gnarled boughs of the barren larches and spruce trees, an open book that has lurched itself shut. To truly understand the nuance of death you must pry the story free.

I had never seen Jan cry until today. The day a magpie died. He insists it was a fox that killed it. He knows so from reading the prints.

"Sad to say. But this is life's way," he tells me, refusing to wipe his good eye. This hardened man unashamed of his tears. It is striking to see. One eye, white as fog and snow, devoid of life, of emotion. The other, the lightest robin's blue, weeping over the gnawed carcass of a gut-torn bird.

"To live, you must die. Even the innocent. But to truly live, you must appreciate life."

"You're talking about the bird?" I ask, head cocked, doing my best to choke back a grin.

"Look. You will see." Jan points up across the neighboring red tin roof. A lone magpie screeches and settles down next to the carcass of its comrade. It bubbles and chirps in a frantic, unbelieving way, nipping at the body and the surrounding snow soaked in claret. I look up to Jan, who nods back down at the bird. The bird that is screaming into the open air, a woeful crow that I have never heard the tiding create.

"Just wait," Jan holds a finger up, strangely, almost smiling, scanning above the roofs and tree lines with his eye. Another magpie shrieks across the clouds and sweeps down upon its companions. Like its friend, it first inspects, and then joins it in the crass squealing. One by one the whole tiding hears the call and circles the dead body, pensive, in reverence. After a few minutes, which Jan and I observe in awestruck silence, the magpies' circle breaks and they begin to disperse.

Back into the barren boughs, the shoddy rooftops, shingles rusted umber and swinging loose. They soar into the clouds with a new respect for life, for freedom. They rip at the beetles and spiders, gnaw grains, and bask their tongues in the tart explosions of discarded fruits of the back streets and grocer's dumpsters. They plunge upon the darting voles and squirrels, which scatter with the lightning-struck adrenaline of self-perseverance. They raid the nests of lesser birds, plunder reflective objects, and shiny trinkets like pirates raising towns for coins of gold. They know they have one life to live. They have seen the splay of blood the sharpened canines of Carpathian foxes produce when connected to their fragile organs. The perfect cuts of straight razors. Their hearts are the snares of the mountains. That marching drum that beats in time or falls behind and out of life's cadence.

"Let us make a fire in the hearth tonight." Jan tells me. "I will show you how to cook a proper stew."

We head indoors under the drip of crooked stalagmite spikes of ice glistening in the light hazing from the kitchen window. The lonely kitchen in this snowbound chalet, on this lifeless block, in this winter city, where the sleeping knight is blanketed in white, high above the valleys and foothills, where creatures kill and are killed, but most of all just try to endure.

***

Dzień dobry, nazywam się Maria Woźniak. I am new to Detroit, Michigan, United States by way of Wrocław. My husband is passed. I am look for good Christian Polish man for to take care of and marry. In my town it has been said I am very beautiful woman. But more than beauty, I can cook! Will relocate for correct man. Send mail to me at address below.

—Maria Woźniak

***

Dear Maria,

My name is Jan. I am writing from Newcastle, Pennsylvania, USA with much interest in meeting your beauty. I am very strong man, handsome, so they say, with good Union job in powder mill where I have saved many men from certain death. Yes, I was once married. My wife? She killed herself, long time ago back in Poland. Though I'm certain she was Russian.

I am from Zakopane, a beautiful town in the Tatra Mountains. I think you might have heard of it, no? There my family still has a home. I spent much time in Krakow and worked in Nowa Huta at Lenin Plant. But USA is my life now. Here I live with my son Piotr in a nice house in a neighborhood by the woods. You will look so good cooking in our home. I can already taste the food.

You must understand I am very man of God. Sunday Church is highest priority! Attached is photo of me in newspaper from when I was hero at the mill. I hope this will entice you to be my bride.

—Jan

***

Jan is sleeping in the passenger seat. It is Piotr's fourteenth birthday. He drives Jan's Ford truck four hours up the highway to the bus station in downtown Detroit to pick up his father's new Polish bride.

Piotr fumbles to hold the steering wheel straight. His palms are sweaty. He tries to merge properly, but it his first time driving on the Interstate. The car jerks across the white dotted lines. Jan wakes up grumbling, wiping drool from his face.

"Almost there?"

"I think so, Dad."

"No one to cook. No one to clean. A man needs a woman, Piotr!" Jan yawns and stretches his arms.

"You had one, Dad," Piotr mutters. Jan pretends not to hear. He crosses his arms and shuts his eyes.

***

We have spent the afternoon in the markets, and now in the kitchen of the chalet, Jan spreads our gathered ingredients across the table, preparing to make a pot of Bigos, *Hunter's Stew.* Dirty dishes pile within the sink. Books, bills, and periodicals are pushed across the counter to make way for slabs of salted meat and bulging green heads of cabbage.

On the wall a clock ticks audibly, only drowned out by the running water or shuffling of bags. A fire flickers a tribal dance in the stone hearth of the connected living room. The burning orange of bottled madness. The stark yellow of unbound energy. A sofa draped in wool blankets watches the flames like an old man staring out into the sea.

A taxidermy buck keeps post above the fireplace, guarding the few framed black and white Soviet-era family photos, with dead eyes that reflect the life of light. Its horns sharp and curved. Ears stiffened and winged out at attention, as if to listen closely to the whispers of the other spirits in the Tatras, stuck between worlds. Somewhat dead but propped alive. A purgatory of body and mind. Watching the living from a hook and nail in the drywall. Sentenced in death to life as a display of human culture.

When Jan cooks, he is surprisingly tender. He patiently instructs me, chopping meat and sauerkraut, whistling fragmented songs, natural as a magpie, like he himself has adopted the language of the corvids.

"I am happy to show you," he admits, dicing onions with a knife, "Piotr never did care to learn. But neither did I, until I had to."

Together, we fry up chopped salt pork and bacon into nuggets and brown the diced onions in the greasy drippings. We rinse and boil sauerkraut and a shredded head of cabbage and combine them with the diced onions and meat nuggets, adding diced and pitted prunes to the hearty mixture. Jan trusts me with the job of cutting two pounds of pork into small cubes, and in an enameled pot we layer the sauerkraut and meat mixtures on top of each other, tossing in the occasional layer of skinned and sliced cherry-smoked kielbasa and chopped mushrooms foraged earlier in my stay, until all the ingredients are gone and a level of browned sauerkraut adorns the very top of the pot in an even plateau.

Jan pours a cup of meat stock and adds it into the stew. He blows a satisfied slide whistle with his pursed lips as he looks down his nose at his handiwork with a cocked head and assured gaze.

"Half an hour medium, and then low for two hours," he tells me. "In the meantime, I wish to show you something."

I breathe in deep the smell of cooked cabbage and onions, the sizzling fat of bacon and pork, while Jan retreats to his room for whatever it is he wishes to share. I can feel my teeth cutting through the tender smoked sausage soaked in stock and bedded in the sweet chewiness of pitted prunes. The smoke lingering off the pot is a premonition to the sustenance of a homemade meal, and the holy rite of bonded labor between grandfather and grandson, the passage of open hearts and shared culture, the turning of the stovetop switches as a subversive act of love, revolutionary in a lineage of estranged fruits hanging from withered branches.

When Jan returns, he is holding an old wooden instrument, vaguely resembling a fiddle. It is carved from a single piece of wood, the main body shaped almost like a canoe, with two filigreed slits for resonance, and a bridge, neck, and four stringed tuning pegs, very much like that of a violin. But Jan does not hold it like a violin. He holds the instrument to his breast and out past his shoulder, left hand upturned and curved around the top of the neck. Then he flashes me a cunning smile, like a young boy about to pull a prank.

"Złóbcoki," he says to me. When he sees I do not understand he explains further. "Or, Gęśle. Old Goral instrument. Like Sabała used to play."

Jan begins to bow the strings, a jaunty, trebly tune of a bygone era, the notes sawing back and forth across the scales with the steadfast gallop of a wild mare. I can almost hear it echoing across the Tatras. He sings a few lines in the white voice glissando, words I do not comprehend, but that are enough to give my spine shuddering chills. When he finishes his piece, he holds out his bow on the final notes across the two lower strings in an octave and draws it out to one final double stop before lowering his head and back into a humble bow.

"Sabała was the Homer of the Tatras," he says proudly, "A highlander, once a highwayman. Then a rover, a storyteller, a legendary musician. His notes told the stories of the mountains. For a people who never had a written history. Wisdom, humor, adventure. Illiterate, but the best writer of his time. And this instrument was the type he played. Here in Zakopane. In these mountains. In these meadows. Here, you try now."

Jan hands me the złóbcoki, and with some effort I attempt to mimic his grip on the instrument. I push it into my left breast and keep it cradled in my palm. But when I move to bow the strings, my right-hand falters, creating the sense of fingernails on a chalkboard, producing a sound much like the screeching of a wounded animal. I cringe. Jan laughs and claps his hands. I hand him back the instrument, and he croons it back into a melancholic song. A bounding tune. Notes the color of an autumn dusk. And once again he is going off with that troublemaker smile, his white glass eye gazing into my soul while the salty smell of simmering fats billows from the stovetop with bursts of dampened crackles.

We refrigerate the stew overnight and as I sleep under the wool blankets to the static calm of the falling snow out the windowpane, I dream of Jan's fiddle and the stories it tells. Jan's fingers launch me across the boundaries of time and place and culture. A warmth rises in my heart when through it all I start to feel at home.

The next day we add red wine and various seasonings to the mixture. By nightfall more kielbasa, mushrooms, and pitted prunes are added and the stew is heated up again. I set up the dining table with rye and black bread, spooning the Bigos into bowls while Jan pours glasses of Jałowcówka, juniper vodka, for us to share.

We clink our drinks together, take deep sips, and begin to spoon steaming bigos into our mouths. We nod and smile, chew, swallow, and sip more vodka, not saying much, but just enjoying each other's company. For the duration of the meal we eat in silence, though I feel comfortable just the same. We have said and shared so much in the act of cooking together that now there is nothing left to do but appreciate the moment.

***

Basia takes me on a walk down Kościeliska Street on a dreary Monday afternoon. Snowfall blankets the roof of old wooden huts which line the block in rustic decay, the mood interrupted by more modern villas. Their open verandas are decorated with potted plants and carved stones, the same color slabs as used in the structures' thick foundations. Arcuate doors and windows compliment the armor of tin shingle roofs, the huts primitive in comparison.

"These huts are the homes of the first highlanders to settle the area," Basia tells me.

"Some way to live," I say, turning my head to examine the entirety of the street.

"Indeed. You know, they used to hike up the mountains from here with their sheep. Heavy packs of food and instruments and supplies hanging off their backs, climbing steep inclines of rugged trails. And they'd go all the way up to the high meadows and camp there. Feast. Play music. Stay there for days. It was a different way of life. It was a different world."

"I could barely make it up that trail on my own," I laugh.

We approach a centuries old wooden church enveloped in trees. Next to it, the stone archway and iron gate of a quaint cemetery riddled with foliage.

"Wow." I stop in my tracks.

"This is my favorite part of town," Basia smiles, pulling me forward by the hand.

"Jan doesn't tell me about this kinda stuff."

"Ha! How is it going with him anyway?"

"You know—I think it's better. I think I'm getting to understand him. We're not so different."

"Eh..." She chuckles.

"What? You don't think so? You never even met the guy."

"Look here," Basia instructs pointing to two separate trees. One is tall and otherwise slender. Pale bark. Branches set up high, bowing out above the church, naked of leaves. The other is shorter. Squat. Pinecones hang from the green nettles of its stubby boughs. "This tall one is a beech tree. This green one is spruce. Are they similar? Yes, they are both trees. Made from the same elements. At home in the forest. But what is different is that the beech trees are natural here in the Tatras. The spruce trees are not."

"Then why are they here?" I ask. My face is visibly put off by Basia's allegory. I'm anxious to understand her point.

"So many of the native beech trees were cut down. The forest destroyed. So, the town began to plant spruces artificially. At first it makes no sense for them to be here. This is not their natural environment. But listen, when the spruce trees transplanted here decompose, their compost gives the soil nutrients to regenerate the forest. These foreign trees are breathing new life into the mountains."

"Why are you telling me this?"

"Ha! You can't see? Because Jan is a beech tree, and you are a spruce!"

"But what does that mean? What are you trying to say?"

"You and Jan aren't the same. But you don't need to be. Here! This is the oldest cemetery in Zakopane! I want you to see!"

"A cemetery? Really?"

"In English, Zakopane means 'Buried'. It is only fitting to take you here," she laughs.

We walk through the gates under the stone arch onto a cobblestone path winding through a woodland sprawl of moss-covered stones. Each carved with names and dates on plots surrounded by wooden totems protruding from the snow like tree stumps, crowned with angled roofs resembling bird houses, or even the shingled tops of the local villas' architecture. A plaque is adorned with a crucifix on each totem, reading birth and death dates among slews of family names.

Some graves are marked by sheets of rusted metal. Others with branches wretched crooked around intricate sculptures. A few bare huts with wooden gnomes. It feels like the entrance to a distant world. One only found within a dream. Crows caw, gliding across the sky. The wind smells of the black smoke drifting in sullen tufts out of brick chimneys nearby. Clouds veil across the midday sun, shading the misty cemetery a complex range of gray.

Bright flowers contrast the spread of white along the soil. They remind me of Jan's crocuses. I grow sentimental observing them. On various graves, photographs of family members are tacked up and posted along with personal mementos, and thick candles, once lit, now seeping tears of melted wax down to their base and onto the stones around them.

"In this cemetery Nazi resistance fighters and war heroes share the same grounds as poets, writers, and musicians. Even Sabała himself is buried in here. Maybe even Jan someday too, huh?"

"C'mon, cut it out, Basia…"

"I'm just kidding. Though, honestly, to be buried here would be quite the honor."

"Can we go somewhere less depressing?"

"If you wish," She says, taking my hand in hers once more, "You know, this is the perfect time of year to check out the slopes."

So, we do.

The afternoon is spent on mechanical lifts up through the mountain woods, under white cap peaks, through hordes of spruces, branches bending low from piles of snow. We ski down moderate slopes, at a distance from each other, cutting diagonally across and back again, steering with our poles as if they were the oars of a ship on some vast frozen ocean. As the red sun sinks below the black cliffs, we have meandered back into town, pub to pub, with glasses of miodunka, tall bottles of Książęce Czerwony, and plates of steaming beef gulasz atop thick potato pancakes. We watch the gorals sing in the tavern rooms while people young and old gather round in accompaniment, clapping hands and clasping each other's shoulders in an intoxicated and satisfied sway.

Before I know it, Basia is kissing me. And in a series of flashes, like photographs, or even missing slides of a film, I am in

Basia's apartment, limbs wrapped around each other. Phallus dipped into rose flower, petals spread, hearts warm, faces gently sweating with both passion and anticipation. Voices soft and cooing into each other's ears. We are the confluence of two rivers flowing out to open water. We are the warmth of summer days held close in memory through the coldest of nights. We are a match struck to flame. The lunar pulls of waves. Purposely rising and falling, just to rise again and crash upon the shore.

Our bodies remain naked. Basia's arm around my torso. The moonlight through the window is enough to illuminate the pages of my moleskin notebook. The roar of the night has faded to a meditative silence. I write and I write, until my eyes flutter shut, my grip grows limp, and the notebook falls from the cradle of my palm.

And still, it is there. The image of the cemetery. The wooden houses of sleeping spirits propped up on posts between stones overgrown with evergreen moss. The curving cobblestone walkway past plots of noble bodies, where I walk nude and barefoot, as a tourist, through the lingering mist of the world of the deceased.

***

Maria is plain and broad shouldered. Her hair is pale. Her eyes, a distant gray. Her nose slopes sharp and her cheeks are round. Her large breasts sag upon her upper belly. She wears long, unflattering black dresses, and dark stockings to hide her legs.

At first Maria does not talk much or show much affection. She cooks. She cleans. And Jan covers her expenses and gives her a decent home. Jan and Maria sleep in two separate beds, feet apart from each other. When they change clothes, they change in separate rooms. The three things that bring them together are church pews, television, and the dinner table.

On Fridays Maria makes a large pot of Żurek to last the weekend. On Sundays before church Maria makes a lunch of herring and potato dumplings. After church she makes dinner of kiełbasa i kapusta. Piotr takes a liking to her. Though money is tight, Maria still feeds him four times a day.

Soon Piotr's shoulders are as broad as his stepmother's. He weighs 230 pounds by the age of sixteen. His face becomes pudgy and circular unlike the thin cut bone structure of his father. Piotr joins the football team. He gets a part time position at the local grocery store packaging and wrapping cuts of meat from the butcher to be displayed for sale in the coolers. He sneaks home the best cuts of beef and sausage for Maria, who cooks them on Sundays for him and Jan.

For some time, Piotr's life feels stable again. There is money in his wallet, meat in the fridge, a mother at home, and glory on the football field. He is a normal kid, just like the rest. He hardly remembers the days of his old mother. The visions are hazy, like a dream, like a field of grass in a fog, wet with dew.

***

"I saw what you wrote about me." Basia tells me. I have finally rolled out of her bed, to meet her in her kitchen in the mid-morning light. I crave coffee and feel foolish for having expected it. Either way, Basia's words catch me off guard.

"What I what?" I stammer, analyzing her downcurved lips and narrowed brows.

"In your little notebook." She pulls it from her pocket and slaps it down on the wooden countertop in front of her.

"You read that?" I groan and wipe my palm across my face.

"Here, let me read it again," she remarks, holding up the moleskin, *"Basia is a somewhat homely young woman. But in that homeliness is a small-town sense of beauty. Hidden by her rather unremarkable sense of style is an idiosyncratic urge for life which can only be birthed in the rural doldrums that deny one a sense of emotionally fulfilling experiences. In the remaining spirit of her youth is an admirable gleam of hope, though it is a pity that her yearning for a greater artistic endeavor does not have much of a leg to stand on. Still, her perseverance is inspiring in itself. I wish to guide her. To show her the way. After all, it is my profession to teach.* Well, that is a total backhanded compliment if I ever saw one! Do you mind telling me what the hell I am supposed to think about that?" My heart sinks in humiliation.

"That was not for you to read!"

"You left it open on the ground."

"They were my private notes!"

"Ha! Well, in a way, I'm glad I read them. It's a good enough signal to no longer waste my time. Your true colors—just another arrogant American."

"Basia—"

"Oh, and I'll have you know," she interjects, slapping the book on the counter once more, "I had recently put out for a work visa in England. Today it has been approved. With my next paycheck I'll be purchasing a plane ticket. To join my father. I don't need your pity. Or your perceptions of hope. I can navigate life just fine all on my own."

"I didn't mean it like that..." I say. But I know there is no convincing her. My self-absorbed drunken notes have solidified who I truly am in her mind.

"It must be so surprising to you what such a homely girl can accomplish." She scoffs. And again, her words cut deep into my chest. One after another. Chopping away at my writing, my ego, my perception of my intellectuality, like an axe sunk into the base of a rotting tree.

"Basia, c'mon. I'm sorry."

"Here," she says, tossing the notebook at my chest, "Take your stories. Take your stories and get out of my life."

"I don't want to leave like this!" I choke back tears, in a mix of self-pity and exasperation.

"If it was a story that you wanted out of this, it is a story that you received. Now please, leave me alone." Her expression is so austere, her tone so commanding, that I have no choice but to grab my things and leave, head held low under the wrath of her leering stare.

I walk through the snowbound streets of Zakopane, the streets I barely know, finding my way by buildings or signs notable enough in recent memory to act as a guide. The air is chilled. My feet crunch in syncopation on the ground. The gray city illuminates in short repetitional bursts as the shades of the clouds drift past the stale light of the late autumn sun.

"What am I doing here?" I mutter under my breath, which spirals visibly in a mist from my lips into the cold. It has been a long time since I have felt this alone.

As I approach the chalet, Jan is outside in his canvas jacket, tossing food onto the patch of ground where his violet crocuses once grew vibrant. Wings flutter. Corvid voices echo screeches. He is soon joined by his tiding. Some gnaw at pieces of food. Others nip at each other in acts of dominance. Another perches on his shoulder, a sentry observing the chaotic display of love sprawled in front of them. Jan sees me in the distance and slowly waves.

I wave back, halfheartedly, though I truly appreciate his presence. I'm happy for him that he has the magpies. In a way he has become one of them. But I have come to realize that my grandfather is not the stark black and white portrait of the old world that I thought him to be. Something more complex. A charcoal image shaded by hand and tool into a profound range of contrasted grays.

***

"Before we go in, there's something I should warn you about," Piotr tells his girlfriend at the doorsteps to Jan's Newcastle home. He and Suzy have recently graduated college at the University of Pittsburgh and Piotr has brought her here to meet his family.

"Uh, oh. What could there possibly be to warn me about?"
Suzy laughs. Her brown hair is feathered, ends curled up and out.
Cheeks rosy. Chestnut eyes bright with life.

"My father...he is, uh...kind of an eccentric."

"Nothing wrong with that. Is he an artist or something?"
Suzy's smile disappears when Piotr can't answer without looking
away.

"Not really," he trails off for a moment, "But what you
should know is he once suffered from cancer of the eye. One of
them had to be removed to save his life. So, in its place is a
prosthetic glass piece."

"I'm sure it will be fine."

"Maybe it's just because he's my dad. But, it's hard to look
at."

"C'mon," Suzy assures him, "He's your dad. I'm sure he will
be just as kind as you. And that's all that really matters."

Piotr nods and turns the key to the latch and then the
knob. With a creak of the door the smells of a homecooked meal
waft out from the house and stimulate their senses. Clanking is
heard from the kitchen. A voice calls out over the trill of a crooner
on the radio.

"Hello? Is that Piotr? Is my boy come home?" It is Maria.

"Hi, Mom!" he yells towards the back room, "I've brought
my girlfriend Suzy over for dinner."

"Your father is in dining room! I am just making to set the table!"

"C'mon," Piotr instructs Suzy. He takes her by the hand through the foyer to the dining room where smoke hangs like morning mist on a lake. Vapor floats from the smoldering tip of Jan's cigar, which is clenched between his yellow toothed jaw, mismatched with silver dental implants and black spots from unattended cavities that attract attention when he smiles to say hello.

"Piotr," Jan beckons in a guttural tone, upon the couple's entrance. He leans back in his chair at the head of the wooden table, covered in plastic, lined with placemats, candles, and white doilies. A long, awkward creak groans out from the legs of his seat as he does so. Suzy does her best to maintain her smile, her bright eyes now wilting like petals of a clipped rose.

"And you are?" Jan says to her. He pulls the cigar out of his mouth, ashes, and hacks a deep-rooted ball of mucus out of his chest which he swallows back down with a sip from a long neck bottle of Iron City Beer.

"I'm Suzy," she tells him, "It's very nice to finally meet you, Jan. Peter has only told me good things about you."

"I always tell Piotr to bring home nice Polish girl. Finally, he bring home beautiful woman." Jan says. Suzy giggles nervously.

"Suzy is an amazing woman, Dad," Piotr interjects, "She studied communications at Pitt with me. She already has some career opportunities lined up for this coming fall. I really think you're going to like her."

"Suzy, tell me, where is your family from?"

"I'm Italian," Suzy shares proudly, "My father is from northern Italy. My mother is Sicilian."

"Hmmm…" Jan considers taking another long drag from his cigar. He stares deep into Suzy's eyes and the gaze of his glass prosthetic is too intense for her to bear. With a throat full of gravel, Jan says two words to her, which are almost as much as he will say to her for the rest of the night. Suzy does her best to hold her stare with him as he says these words. But his eye is almost mesmerizing.

"Spaghetti Bender."

"Dad!" Piotr yells. But before he can correct his father, Maria bursts into the dining room with a tray of ham, sauerkraut, and beet and cucumber salads.

"Dinner ready!" she coos in a sing song voice.

The family eats their dinner together in silence. The squishing of teeth mushing and crunching on food gargles out over the clinking of silverware on china plates and the ice rattling in glasses of water and kompot. Each audible swallow sinks with a bubbling gulp. Piotr is used to this. Suzy, not so much. She nudges him under the table.

"Peter," she says, "Aren't you going to tell them?"

"I will. I will…"

"Tell what?" Maria pries.

"Uh, well..." He hesitates, catching Jan's overcast stare.

"C'mon, Peter. Tell them."

"Please do," Maria adds.

"Well, Mom. Dad. Suzy and I would like to announce—we are going to be getting married."

Maria bursts with an expression of joy. She comes around the table and clutches Piotr to her breasts, kissing him on the head. Likewise, she turns to Suzy and embraces her, welcoming her into the family. Jan gets up from his seat too. Though he does so more violently, causing a stir.

"Fine," he says, "Get married to greaseball. If that is what you want. But I have learned hard way not to trust such gypsies." And with this, he takes what is left of his beer and heads to the living room and watches the TV from a paisley patterned sofa cased with plastic and draped with a white knit blanket.

Suzy and Piotr are speechless, though they couldn't get in a word if they wanted to. Maria has their faces buried into her sagging bosoms in an embrace so loving and welcoming that no amount of ignorance in the world would be allowed to penetrate.

***

"Unlucky in love, eh?" Jan says to me. We are sitting on his sofa, watching the flames of the hearth, eyes reflecting the orange, skin lit with warmth. The taxidermy buck is frozen in time, staring out of the face of its fate. I examine the old photos framed below it, propped up on the mantel's gray slab of stone.

On the coffee table are steaming bowls of polewka piwna, beer soup that Jan has guided me to prepare.

"Yup, you could say that," I tell him. "I don't know. More so just lonely, I guess."

"Loneliness," he says as if considering the word's meaning, "I too know loneliness."

"But Jan, not to be this way, but you sort of chose to be alone, didn't you?"

"Let me tell you something about this town—when the Poles first came to the Tatras, they believed there was gold in these mountains. They intended to mine the Carpathians for all the gold they could find. They believed they would be rich. And yes, there was gold. *Some.* But not a considerable amount. More than that, there was iron ore. Not as desirable. But still, they stayed. In the absence of gold, they committed to mining the iron ore and coal. It was *what it was.* And when Maria and I returned to Poland, I swore I would find the gold in these mountains that I remembered there to be in my youth. What I found was loneliness. Then Maria passed. What I have are my sroka, and now you. And of course, my memories..."

Jan nods up to the photos on the mantel. With a groan he lifts himself from the sofa and approaches the frames. Out the window the snowfall is heavy. In the lull of conversation all that can be heard is the creaking of the walls, the howl of the wind, and the crackling pop of billowing flames.

"This is Maria," Jan says holding up a photo of his late wife. I nod, hardly remembering her from my younger years. "But she was not my first wife."

"You were remarried?"

"Your father's true mother. My first wife. Her, I keep no photos of."

"You didn't love her?"

"It was deeper than that. Here look. I show you. My mother, Magda. My father, Krzysztof." His parents are portraits of stoicism, broad shoulders, large square heads, faces in a natural frown. His father in an oversized suit. His mother in an austere black dress. They stand in front of the chalet, ghosts of a lost generation, white as snow, black as crows, gray as a hazy memory. But there is a red to the image as well. One I can't see at face value. I just have to know it to be so. It is the same red that flows through the veins of all those in our family tree, binding us together whether we wish it to or not.

"So serious," I remark with a smirk. Jan does not see the humor.

"We lived through World War. Communism. Soviet Union. Life was a challenge. As serious as they were, I knew them to be good people. Good, good people," he begins to trail off, lost in the photographs with an expression of longing. He joins me on the sofa and puts his hand on my shoulder. "I am happy you are here," he tells me. "I am grateful."

"But Jan," I say, "You still haven't told me why you left us. You just missed this place so much? So much you stayed here all these years? Without us?" A tear drops from Jan's good eye. He reaches into the breast pocket of his shirt and pulls out a golden ring topped with a diamond stud. I recognize it to be the same ring that we caught the magpie fiddling with in the garden earlier in the fall.

"You want to know why I'm here. I tell you. I tell you the whole story. But look. Look into my eyes. See me. What I have to say. And don't look away. Just look." He fiddles with the ring in his palms as he talks.

Jan begins to tell me his story. The whole story. I stare into his white glass eye. It truly is like a crystal ball. Clouded. Highlighted with the glow of the hearth's embers. In his eyes I see everything. Like a storybook. Like the rattling illumination of a film projector against a blank wall in a room as dark as the buried secrets of shattered men. But Jan's stories are no longer his secrets. He tells me everything. The night rages on with sawing wind and glacial frost. Our steaming soups grow cold and we've barely touched them. There is just so much more to learn.

***

Jan stands in front of Piotr in the back room of St. Mary's Roman Catholic Church holding the gold band of a diamond ring up to his son's face. Bells chime out in a resplendent clamor from inside the steeple as guests shuffle through the arched doors, down the aisle, and into the pews. Towards the rafters in the front of the hall, an organist presses keys and pedals into piping bursts of divine harmonies that echo and sustain throughout the surrounding room, decorated with stations of the crucifixion, and somber stained-glass portraits of bygone saints and the blessed virgin.

"It was your mother's," Jan tells him. "Your real mother."

"Dad—" begins Piotr, but Jan interrupts him.

"Give it to Suzy," he says. "And just know this—know that I am sorry." He hands Piotr the ring and they draw into a warm embrace.

Piotr turns and walks through the door to the wedding ceremony and the celebration of love spirals into nights of scattered stars hung like paintings through the milky cosmos. The moon's cycles pass with the set and rise of the summer sun, flames beating like the pulse of lover's hearts, steady, heavy, in rhythm with the breath of the universe.

The earth has turned so fast that Piotr has hardly had time to catch up to the present, where Suzy is giving birth in Allegheny General Hospital. The doctor's return from the hours of labor with a solemn expression and the crying body of a newborn baby boy. He is overwhelmed by the rawness of existence and the blinding nature of the hospital lights. And he is beautiful. But this is followed by the conveyance of regret and the condolences for the tragedy of the mother who just lost her life in giving life to the child.

Piotr's tears flow the river of consciousness, that which always rips towards the greater body of incorporeal water, whether straight and narrow or straying many miles off direction in search of something close to solace. But even more, for a semblance of meaning. Of truth.

Before he knows it, his son is a young boy. He watches him play with toy trains across the rug of Jan's living room, while Jan himself learns the news of the fall of the Soviets on his small box television which he has kept since the late nights of John Wayne and whiskey when Piotr was just a child.

The Poles on TV are lining up down the span of two blocks to try their first taste of McDonald's hamburgers. Not because they believe the burgers will be good. But because this is the first taste of a new way of the world. Piotr is talking to Jan, but he is entranced in the flashes of light. The footage of his old country. His old life, with his wife, long gone. And he knows deep down he wishes to be back home. He always has.

Jan and Maria stop by Piotr's apartment before they depart. Anxiousness turns to forced conversation, turns to arguments, then awkwardness. Jan shuts himself in Piotr's room and locks the door.

"C'mon, Mom," Piotr says, "What is all this? Why? You have a grandchild here!"

"My Piotr," she says softly, "This is what your father needs to do. You know he always love you."

When Jan returns from Piotr's bedroom, having calmed himself down, there is something off about the way he acts. He is anxious to leave. He hugs his grandson, kisses his forehead, and then holds Piotr tightly.

"I'm sorry, Żabko," he whispers into his son's ear.

"Then just stay," Piotr sighs.

"That is not what I mean..."

Weeks after his parents are gone, the birthday of Piotr's son is arriving. A day shrouded in mourning and bitterness. Nostalgic of Suzy, Piotr retrieves the jewelry box holding Suzy's wedding ring, and he finds it to be gone. At first, he scours his apartment, a frantic mess. Manic. But then he pieces together the memories of Jan. The last other person to be in his room. And he finally understands what his father meant by "Sorry."

***

"So, this is why you and Dad don't talk?" I stammer, "Because you couldn't care less about your family? Too absorbed in yourself. In your own problems. This is why you were never around?"

"Please—" Jan pleads, trying to stop me from standing up. In his face is an expression of vulnerability and weakness I've never known his features to wear. "Please, understand!"

"Well, it seems I've got my answers."

"Answers?"

"The reason I came. It's crystal clear. I think I'm ready to go home now."

"Right now?"

"Maybe tomorrow," I say, throwing on my jacket and heading towards the front door.

"Then where are you going?"

"I'm going for a beer."

Jan follows me through the kitchen, but I am already in the foyer slipping on my shoes. I open the door and head outside into the slanted downpour of sleet and snow. I slip on the ice atop the stones of the front steps and curse incoherently,

71

popping my knee and almost falling back onto my ass. I grumble to myself as I trudge through the violent haze of black and white.

"Wait!" he calls after me. "I'm sorry!" I do not look back.

"Jan," I shout over the spires of wind, "Out of all the times you've said that to your family over the years, do you think even once you really meant it?"

I am off through the side yards and alleyways when I hear Jan's voice cry out in the night one last time. I cannot decipher his words, nor do I care to give him the time of day. I take the back streets to Café Piano and enter the door to the usual scene of casual desolation.

Basia groans when she sees me. Her regular, Mateusz sits in a swing on the other side of the counter. The seat in which he always sits. She shoots him a look and he shakes his head. He takes a swig of his vodka and slams the glass upside down on the bar.

"Basia, daj mi piwo! Give me a beer!" I shout.

"Are you serious right now?" she replies, face wrinkled with disgust.

"My family's fucked. Jan betrayed us. I don't give a shit about anything right now. I'm booking a return flight home first thing in the morning. C'mon, one last beer. Just one. Maybe two!"

Basia starts to speak, but Mateusz shoots up from his swing and interrupts.

"Can't you see she doesn't want to talk to you, głupek? Much less serve you alcohol! You, the tough guy who thinks he can drink Spirytus! Are you feeling tough tonight? Tak?" I put up my hands in defense as Mateusz shoves me back and into the wall. I can tell he has wanted to do this since the first day we met. Though I can't tell who he is doing this for more, Basia or himself. He shoves me again and Basia screams.

"Enough! Stop! Enough! No violence! Mateusz! Out with you! Please!"

"Really?" he asks dumbfounded.

"Yes, really!" Basia commands. "Let me talk to him, alone. Please!"

Mateusz protests more, but she continues to shut him down. He concedes and grabs his coat, cursing the both of us under his breath as he sulks out the door into the ice and snow. I approach the bar and Basia has poured me a beer. I take a seat in a swing and grab my pint. Basia pours herself a pint too and comes around the bar to sit with me.

"It's closing time anyway," she reasons, "And only Mateusz has come in today with this rotten weather."

"Look, Basia," I tell her, "I'm an idiot. I've been an idiot. It seems I come from a whole family, a long line of idiots. And I know words like this sometimes come off as empty, but for what it's worth I'm sorry for the way I was. Just another arrogant, self-absorbed American."

"It's your last night here then, eh?" Basia holds up her glass to me, "Then let's have a drink. Or two. For what it's worth…" We clink our pints together. Her lips curve in a gentle smile. Basia pats her hand on my shoulders, sips, and sets down her beer. "All is forgiven," she tells me. "And look, we are both about to go on quite the journey. Each in our own way."

"This may sound stupid," I say, "But will you write to me? When you are in England, that is."

"Hmmm," she considers, "I may write *about* you. But to you? Only time will decide."

"Fair enough."

"Don't think about that now though. The past. The future. Right now, let us just enjoy this present moment." And we do.

We sip draughts and glasses of vodka, rocking back and forth in our barstool swings. We shift between small talk and discussions of the world at large, but through our inebriation our focus is almost always brought back on each other. The night goes on and drunken embraces turn to kisses, to drinking toasts drawn out as bar-lit manifestos.

The morning arrives with the crack of sunrays through the back patio windows and we find ourselves to have passed out in each other's arms on Café Piano's floor, alongside puddles of spilled beer, eyes bloodshot, hair a mess, still wearing all our clothes. Outside, the snow has ceased. A new day has come, and with it, a certain calm.

"Goodbye," I kiss Basia. Not on the lips, but on her forehead, as her eyes flutter open and then back into her dreams. She whispers something I can't understand and rolls over with her head in her hands. I leave her there, on the floor of the bar. And, in a way, leave part of myself back inside that room.

***

I am not dreaming. Jan's body is laying near the stones of the front steps of his home, bedded in a blanket of snow. The door to the chalet is thrown open, sliding loose, rocking back and forth in the wind. I see Jan there, soiled clothes, grim face pale white, bruised black, purple, and blue. His mouth is held open, up in the air, tongue wretched frozen in the cold under the blood orange sun on this cloudless day. Something terrible has happened. I call an ambulance, break down, and cry.

I remember him trying to follow me. I remember the icy steps. How I popped my knee and almost completely lost my footing on the stones. I now understand the muffled cry in the night as I trudged to the café. The cry I heard but refused to acknowledge. The cry coming from the man who I now know to have been truly sorry.

As I wait for the EMTs to arrive, something odd happens, though I don't think much of it at first. A bird is singing on a nearby roof. It glides down to Jan's lifeless body, and I realize it to be a magpie. The magpie twitches its head, opens its wings, chirps in anxiety. It hops and hobbles around Jan, examining him from head to toe. Glass eye, to black winter boots. And when this examination is done, it lets out a resounding series of woeful screeches. In a matter of minutes, the tiding is upon us.

Black and white feathers. They come dressed for the funeral. They surround Jan's body in a screeching cacophony. I wipe tears from my eyes, now struck with awe. I remember the day the fox killed their brethren. The ceremony that proceeded. They treat Jan like one of their own. They mourn him. Before I can fully process what is going on they have taken off. Back into the rooftops, the naked trees, the snow fallen gardens, and stacks of firewood lining the old verandas.

An ambulance arrives and Jan is taken to the nearest hospital. I wait out front for a taxi to bring me there in tow. As I do so, I stare into the snow, imagining the garden of crocuses that once grew. And the dream, or more so, the premonition. But something shining catches my eye. Reflecting off the rays of sun. I do a double take, squinting curiously as I approach. And when I get closer, I see it is the diamond on the gold banded wedding ring.

I pick it up, holding it before my face. I consider what this means to me. Where it has been. Who has worn it. What this symbol and its associated owners have endured. I close my palm tight around the ring and slip it into my pocket. I know I must call my family back home.

In the taxi cab, I don't have much to say to the driver. I rest my head on the window and stare out at the countryside doing my best to stifle my tears. Out of all the intrusive thoughts concerning me, crossing my mind, something Basia said to me sticks out as important.

Jan is a beech tree, and you are a spruce!

The beech trees are natural in the Tatras. But so many of them have been chopped away. The spruce, transplanted, are brought here to regenerate the forest. For most of the ride towards the hospital, I consider this. And by the time I am paying my fare, I know inside that I intend to stay.

I go to bed at night in Jan's chalet. An eerie calm has taken over the cottage. For hours I lay awake, reimagining Jan's life, playing it back through my head. I hear the sad songs on his fiddle. I smell the homecooked stews. I see the stoic faces of bygone generations. I never knew them but I feel closer to them than ever. And then I think of the family that I do know.

Soon they will be somewhere above the Atlantic. Flying over one by one. They have left the scattered lights of their towns and cities in the wake of the sunset behind them. Now they head across the world in pitch darkness, to chase its rise. And to pay their respects. To the man who showed me the extraordinary color found in the contrast of black and white.

***

Mid-afternoon, Jan is sitting at the desk in the bedroom of his family's cottage. He has pen and paper at hand, composing a letter to his son. A tear drips upon the sheet, diluting the black of the ink across the page. He grunts in frustration and balls the paper up before tossing it back over his shoulder and slamming his fist down onto the wooden surface. Jan sniffles and lays his head into his crossed arms.

When the peak of his self-pity has subsided, Jan heads down the stairs into his living room and gathers his Złóbcoki fiddle by the hearth. "Like Sabała," he assures himself under his breath. He brings the instrument out to the stone slabs that make up his front stoop and begins to play.

Jan is lost in the music and equally lost in his memories. He hardly notices at first when a bird hops towards him with curious chirps, twisting its head to each side while fluttering its wings. The bird lets out a greater caw, surprising Jan enough to look up from his Złóbcoki.

"Sroka," he smiles, "So nice to meet you, little friend..."

The more he plays, the more the magpie sings along and totters about. Soon from the boughs of the golden larch the whole tiding swoops in to greet him. He brings them seeds, pieces of fruit, and bread to nip at in the grass. While they feast, he bows his fiddle and closes his eyes, the notes of the song breaking the barrier of language between human and beast.

The tune swells into the autumn air, past the gloomy smoke of the chalet's brick chimneys and drifting yellow leaves. The vibrations of strings echo across the Tatras, where the ochre flora decays to give birth to luscious green. Jan smiles, wider this time. He can feel it in his chest. All hearts beat in rhythm. As one song. One single verse.

Thank You

First and foremost, I would like to thank Emily Perkovich, Vita Lerman, and the rest of the staff at Querencia Press for their work in publishing this manuscript. I would also like to thank my family, my wife Ayanni, and my friends, Spencer and Scott for guiding me and being supportive of my life in writing. Lastly, I would like to thank author, Patrick Michael Finn, for being a major advocate of my work, and showing me the ropes of the literary world.